Have Fun, Be Healthy and Play
Skating

Pamela Ashley Spuehler

Have Fun, Be Healthy and Play
Copyright © 2021 by Pamela Ashley Spuehler

All rights reserved. No part of this publication may be reproduced, distributed, or transmitted in any form or by any means, including photocopying, recording, or other electronic or mechanical methods, without the prior written permission of the author, except in the case of brief quotations embodied in critical reviews and certain other non-commercial uses permitted by copyright law.

Tellwell Talent
www.tellwell.ca

ISBN
978-0-2288-5950-5 (Hardcover)
978-0-2288-5949-9 (Paperback)

This book is dedicated to my Mom and Dad for their constant encouragement and support in making so many of my dreams and goals a reality.

Breathing in cold air and feeling wind on our face, We take a sip of water before we have a little race.

Our muscles are loose and ready to skate,
Mentally preparing with a steady heart rate.

Feeling our heart pound rapidly in our chest,
Breathing real heavy, our bodies
will soon need a rest.

Skating gets our blood pumping
and helps our muscles grow,
An anaerobic workout where we
skate both fast and slow.

Try these exercises to help you be stronger.
Exercise 1: Lateral bounds (AKA Skaters),
Exercise 2: mountain climbers

Made in United States
North Haven, CT
14 December 2021